JULES FEIFFER

Michael di Capua Books

Hyperion Books for Children

FOR ELIZABETH SCALABRINI

Copyright © 2001 by Jules Feiffer   Library of Congress catalog card number: 2001088920   Designed by Steve Scott   First edition, 2001

Someone's calling Bobby.

I'm not Bobby.

I'm a lion.

But maybe I used to be Bobby.

She's always calling "Bobby, Bobby, Bobby!"
all the time. I get tired of it.

I'm an airplane.

Now I'm a dinosaur.

Bobby!

Nobody goes around calling
"Dinosaur, Dinosaur, Dinosaur!" all the time.

Nobody says, "Come here, Dinosaur!"
They say, "Go way, Dinosaur."

Better not call me again because
I'm a monster.

You know what a monster does when
you yell "Come here!" at him?

A monster comes all right.

And it tears you to pieces.

Unless I come to save you.

I kill the monster with one fist.

Because I'm a giant.

Lucky for you I'm not Bobby,
who couldn't kill a monster.

Even a sick, weak, puny monster.

Thats' it, Bobby!

I'm not Bobby.

huff puff

come back here, young man!

No! I'm Bobby riding a horse.

I'm a race car that Bobby's driving.

I'm an eagle that's rescued Bobby.

huff puff

can't
anyone
huff puff
catch
Bobby?
huff puff
Cousin Frank?
huff puff
Aunt Sally?

I'm a spaceship carrying
Bobby into outer space.

You're in big trouble now, young man!

I can't hear a word she's yelling because I'm halfway to Mars.

You'll come home when you're hungry and then you're going to get it!

If I could hear you, I'd worry.
Anyhow, you're never hungry on Mars.

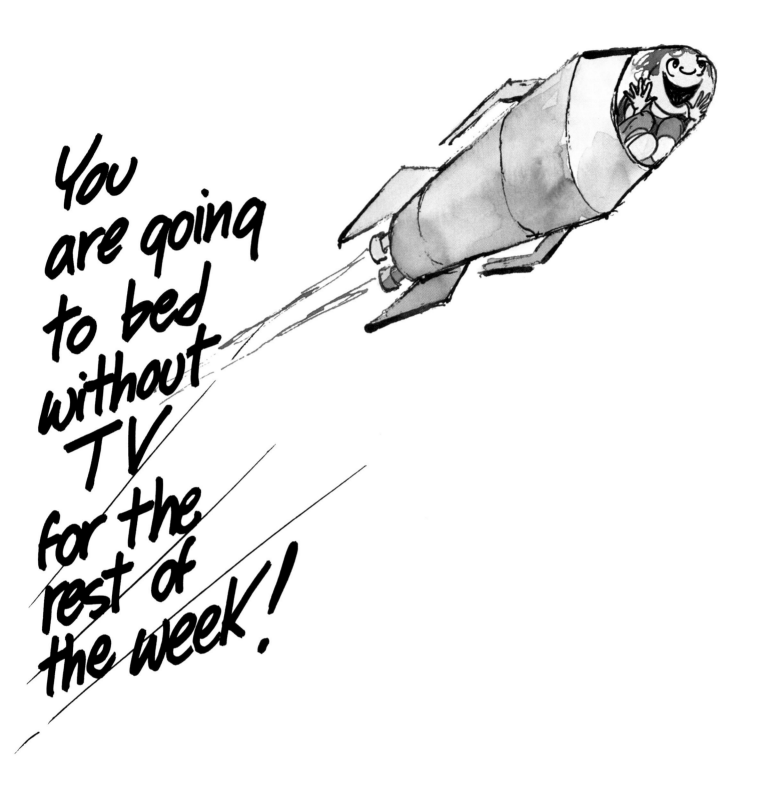

You are going to bed without TV for the rest of the week!

Mars has TV. Every channel. I can watch my shows and she won't even know it.

You have a lot of learning to do, young man!

SLAM

Wow!
I'm alone in space.

This is what I wanted my whole life!

I'm hungry. Space is stupid.

I'm a lion again.

I'll put on a Bobby face

so they don't know I'm a lion.

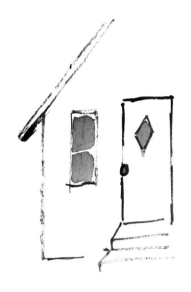

I'll go home.

They'll think I'm Bobby. They'll feed me.

And then they better let me watch TV.

Or I'll eat them.

E
Fei

DATE DUE

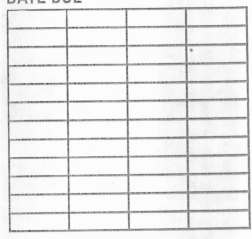

E
Fei   Feiffer, Jules
            I'm Not Bobby